E
MCP

McPhail, David M.

Annie & Co.

$13.45

DATE	
JAN 28 1992	DEC 15 1992
FEB 25 1992	
MAR 1 2 1992	JAN 1 2 1993
APR 9 1992	FEB 8 1993
APR 2 1 1992	MAR 9 1993
MAY -5 1992	APR 1 4 1993
MAY 2 0 1992	MAY 2 9 1993
AUG 0 4 1992	JUN 2 3 1993
	SEP 1 5 1993
OCT 3- 1992	SEP 2 9 1993
	OCT 1 2 1993

**$5.00 FEE PLUS FULL PRICE
FOR EACH ITEM LOST**

© THE BAKER & TAYLOR CO.

ANNIE & Co.

Story and Pictures by
DAVID McPHAIL

Henry Holt and Company　·　*New York*

To Gabes—the original Annie

Once there was a little girl named Annie who lived with her family above her father's repair shop.

The repair shop was filled with all manner of things waiting to be fixed: toasters, lamps, chairs, radios, picture frames, pencil sharpeners, bicycles, musical instruments, and toys.

In the yard in front of the shop were automobiles, trucks, tractors, wagons, hay rakes, and the wings, propeller, and tail of an airplane. They wouldn't fit inside.

Annie spent most of her time watching her father repair things. Annie was a good learner. She had only to watch her father fix something—once—and she knew by heart how to do it herself.

For her sixth birthday Annie's father gave her a tool chest of her own. On the lid, Annie's name was painted in gold.

With her new tools Annie worked right alongside her father. While he nailed the loose shoe of Abner Withers's mare, Annie fixed the bent wheel of Jimmy Withers's wagon.

"There isn't much you can't fix," Annie's father told her one day. "And the world is chockfull of things that need fixing."

For a long time Annie thought about what her father had said. Finally she knew what she wanted to do.

"I want to go out in the world and fix what needs fixing."

At first her father was against the idea, but he could see the determination in her eyes, and at last he relented.

He helped Annie fix up her pony cart.

They made a place for Annie's tool chest and packed a picnic basket with bread, cheese, and fruit, which Annie's mother covered with a new red bandanna. Then Annie painted a sign that read ANNIE & CO. WE FIX ANYTHING, and nailed it to the front of the cart.

Early the next morning Annie hitched her pony, Bub, up to the cart and kissed her father and mother good-bye. Then, with her cat, Bill, sitting on the seat beside her, Annie called, "Get-up, Bub!" and the pony cart rumbled and swayed down the road and disappeared from view.

Annie sat on the swaying seat, singing a song of the open road:

> *"Fix it, fix it,*   *Whack it, crack it,*
> *We can fix it,*   *Even smack it—*
> *We can fix it,*   *We can fix it,*
> *Yes, we can.*   *Yes, we can."*

Annie and Company were passing a big white house when they heard a sound so awful that Bub reared up and almost tipped the cart over.

"Whoa, Bub—easy!" called Annie. She jumped to the ground and climbed up on the front gate to see what was making that sound.

"What's that noise?" she asked a little girl who was holding a pink parasol.

"A famous cellist is supposed to be playing pretty music for my birthday party," whined the girl, "but instead he's making the most absolutely horrid noise!"

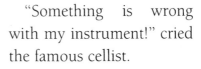

"Something is wrong with my instrument!" cried the famous cellist.

"Maybe I can fix it," said Annie, swinging into the yard.

She picked up the cello and shook it. Then she peered inside.

"Aha!" she exclaimed. "I see what the trouble is."

She went to the cart and returned a moment later with some string, a piece of cheese, and her cat, Bill. Annie tied one end of the string to the cheese and lowered it into the cello. When she pulled the string back out, a little gray mouse was clinging to the cheese . . . nibbling contentedly. But when it caught sight of Bill, the mouse ran and hid under the front steps of the house.

"Try it now," said Annie to the cellist, who took his bow and struck up.

Immediately the air was filled with the sweetest, most wonderful music imaginable.

"For you, dear girl," the proud cellist said to Annie.

As she and Bill were leaving, the little girl thanked Annie and handed her the pink parasol.

"Thanks. I'll save it for a rainy day," said Annie, and she went on her way.

Soon Annie and Company came to a crossroads, where a clown was attempting to entertain a crowd of children.

Try as he might, however, the clown could not make the children laugh. In desperation, he reached into his bag of tricks and pulled out a mouse puppet.

Usually the mouse puppet was a big hit. But not this time. These children didn't even smile. The clown was ready to give up. Then Bill arrived. Bill had seen one mouse get away, and he was determined this one wouldn't. He crouched on the edge of the wagon seat, flattened his ears, wiggled his behind—and sprang!

Over the heads of the children he flew and grabbed right onto that mouse.

Oh, there was a terrible row!

The clown and the mouse—with Bill holding tight—rolled around on the ground. The children howled gleefully.

They laughed so hard they cried, and fell back on the grass holding their sides. Finally Bill wrestled the mouse away from the clown.

"Give it back, Bill," scolded Annie.

"He can keep it," said the clown, staggering to his feet. "He saved the day for me. I was beginning to think that nothing could make those kids laugh."

Then the clown handed Annie a pair of rose-colored glasses with a big rubber nose attached. "Here's something for you," he said.

Annie thanked the clown, placed the glasses under the seat, and drove away.

Later that morning they rode into a small town. The town was deserted except for a boy leaning against a tree.

"Where is everybody?" Annie asked.

"It's town-meeting day," the boy explained, "but the people won't come until the bell in the tower rings—and the bell can't ring, because the clapper is broken!"

"Sounds serious," said Annie. "But I think I can help."

She unhitched Bub and led him through the doorway of the town hall and up the stairs to the belfry.

"How many times would you like the bell to ring?" Annie called down.

"Any number at all," the boy called back. "Five or six should do!"

Bub turned backside to the bell and gave it a wicked kick.

"Bong!" went the bell.

Bub kicked again—Bong!—and again.

"Bong! BONG!" the bell chimed.

A few more kicks and the job was done. By the time Annie and Bub came down from the tower, the streets were filled with people.

Everyone stood and cheered Annie and Bub.

The mayor presented Annie with a chocolate cake, and then he tied a shiny silk ribbon around Bub's neck. Attached to the ribbon was a gleaming gold bell.

"In appreciation," said the mayor.

Annie hitched Bub back up to the cart. She carefully set the cake on top of her picnic basket, then hollered, "Get up, Bub!" The cart lurched once and wobbled away.

Not far out of town Annie steered the cart to the side of the road.

"We'll stop here for lunch," she said. She filled Bub's feed bag with oats and a slice of cake. Then she lifted the picnic basket out of the cart and sat down to eat.

Annie and Bill and Bub were just finishing their lunch when a goose tumbled from the sky and landed with a thud at Annie's feet.

Gently Annie lifted the poor creature onto her lap. Upon careful examination, Annie discovered that the goose had a broken wing.

"I've never fixed a broken wing," she told the goose. "Yours will be the first."

With some sticks and some strips of cloth, Annie made a splint. Then she tied the bandanna her mother had given her around the goose's neck to hold the wing while it healed.

Annie boosted the goose up onto the wagon seat between her and Bill.

"Let's go, Bub," she called.

They hadn't gone far when they came upon an old man shuffling along the road.

"*Honk, honk,*" cried the goose.

The old man moved out of the way.

"Woe is me," he moaned.

"Can we be of service?" asked Annie. "Can we fix anything?"

"I doubt it," said the old man.

"Let us try," said Annie. "Already we've fixed a cello, a bell, and a broken wing."

"But can you make old bones new?" muttered the old man. "Can you make dull eyes bright?"

"Sure can," said Annie. "Climb up here and give those old bones a rest."

Bill and the goose slid over to make room. Annie reached under the seat and pulled out the rose-colored glasses.

"Try these," she said.

The old man put the glasses on.

"This is amazing!" he chuckled. "My bones feel younger already, and these glasses make a world of difference."

Annie smiled, and Bub clopped along in time to the raindrops that had just begun to fall.

It was raining hard as they crossed a rickety bridge. On the bridge stood a young couple. They seemed to be crying, though in the pouring rain it was hard to tell.

"What's wrong?" Annie asked.

"Everything," sighed the young woman. "We were supposed to be married, but then the rain came . . . and the cake got washed away . . ."

"And not a single guest showed up," continued the young man. "Not even the preacher!"

"Maybe we can help," said Annie. "We can fix just about anything."

She handed the umbrella to the goose, who held it steadily over the young couple with her one good wing.

"We have some cake left over from lunch," said Annie, "and as you can see, you have plenty of guests."

"But we still don't have anyone to marry us," the young woman pointed out.

"As captain of this cart," declared Annie, "I can marry you!" And she did.

During the ceremony, Bub's bell pealed softly and the sun broke through the clouds. Then the preacher and the musicians arrived and the festivities began. The celebration continued into the late afternoon.

The sun was setting when Annie said to Bill, "Time for us to go."

The old man's bones never felt better, so he decided to stay and dance some more.

"You can keep the glasses," Annie told him.

The goose waded into the stream and paddled off. She couldn't fly but she sure could swim, and in a moment she was gone.

Annie and Bill climbed back into the pony cart.

Annie whistled to Bub, and they were on their way once more.

As they drove along, the moon came up and the stars came out.

Bill snuggled up to Annie and began to purr softly.

Annie thought about her father, and smiled. He was right. The world was full of things that needed fixing, and Annie and Company had fixed more than a few of them that day.

Then Annie closed her eyes and went to sleep.

Bub would take them home.

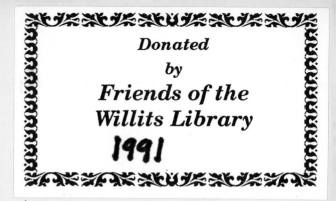
Copyright © 1991 by David McPhail
All rights reserved, including the right to reproduce
this book or portions thereof in any form.
Published by Henry Holt and Company, Inc.,
115 West 18th Street, New York, New York 10011.
Published in Canada by Fitzhenry & Whiteside Limited,
195 Allstate Parkway, Markham, Ontario L3R 4T8.

Library of Congress Cataloging-in-Publication Data
McPhail, David M.
Annie & Co.
Summary: When her father tells her that the world is
full of things that need fixing, young Annie, with her
cat and horse, sets out to fix them.
1. Children's stories, American. [1. Repairing—
Fiction] I. Title.
PZ7.M2427Fic 1984   [E]   84-9084
Trade ISBN: 0-8050-1596-5
Reinforced Library Binding ISBN: 0-8050-1686-4

Printed in the United States of America

1 3 5 7 9 10 8 6 4 2